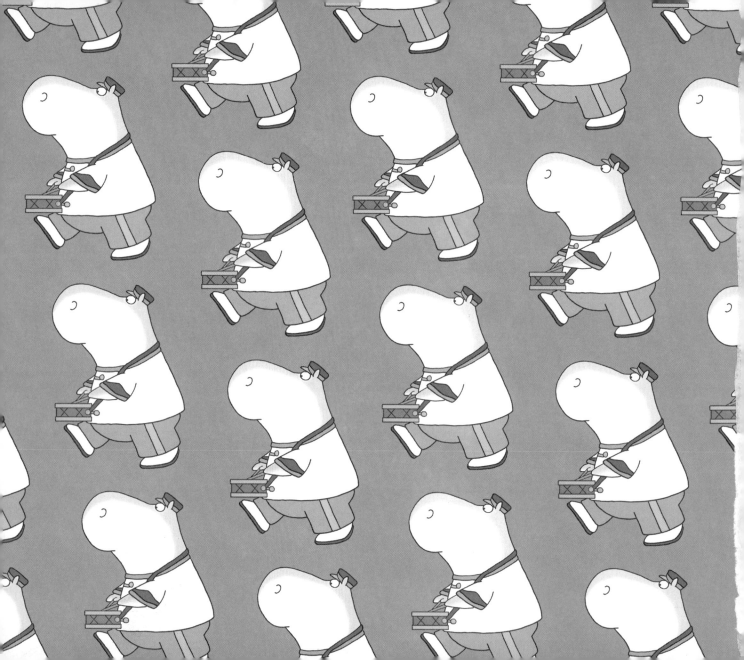

CHRISTMAS PARADE

CHRISTMAS PARADE

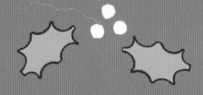

by Sandra Boynton

To the amazing Sarah Getz

SIMON AND SCHUSTER

First published in Great Britain in 2012 by Simon and Schuster UK Ltd • 1st Floor, 222 Gray's Inn Road, London, WC1X 8HB • A CBS Company
Originally published in 2012 by Little Simon, an imprint of Simon and Schuster Children's Publishing Division, New York • Copyright © 2011, 2012 by Sandra Boynton
All rights reserved, including the right of reproduction in whole or in part in any form • A CIP catalogue record for this book is available from the British Library upon request
www.sandraboynton.com • ISBN: 978-0-85707-988-6 • Printed in the U.S.A • 10 9 8 7 6 5 4 3 2 1

BOOM biddy
BOOM BO
Biddy BOOM
biddy BOOM

4

BOOM biddy OM BOOM! biddy BOOM BOOM BOOM!

What's that noise filling the room?

I think that's the sound of the

CHRISTMAS PARADE!

Run to
the window!

Pull up
the shade!

YES!

First comes the elephant
marching along
with a

BOOM–biddy
BOOM–biddy

steady and strong.

And next come the chickens

with silver bassoons...

...followed by piggies
with Christmas balloons.

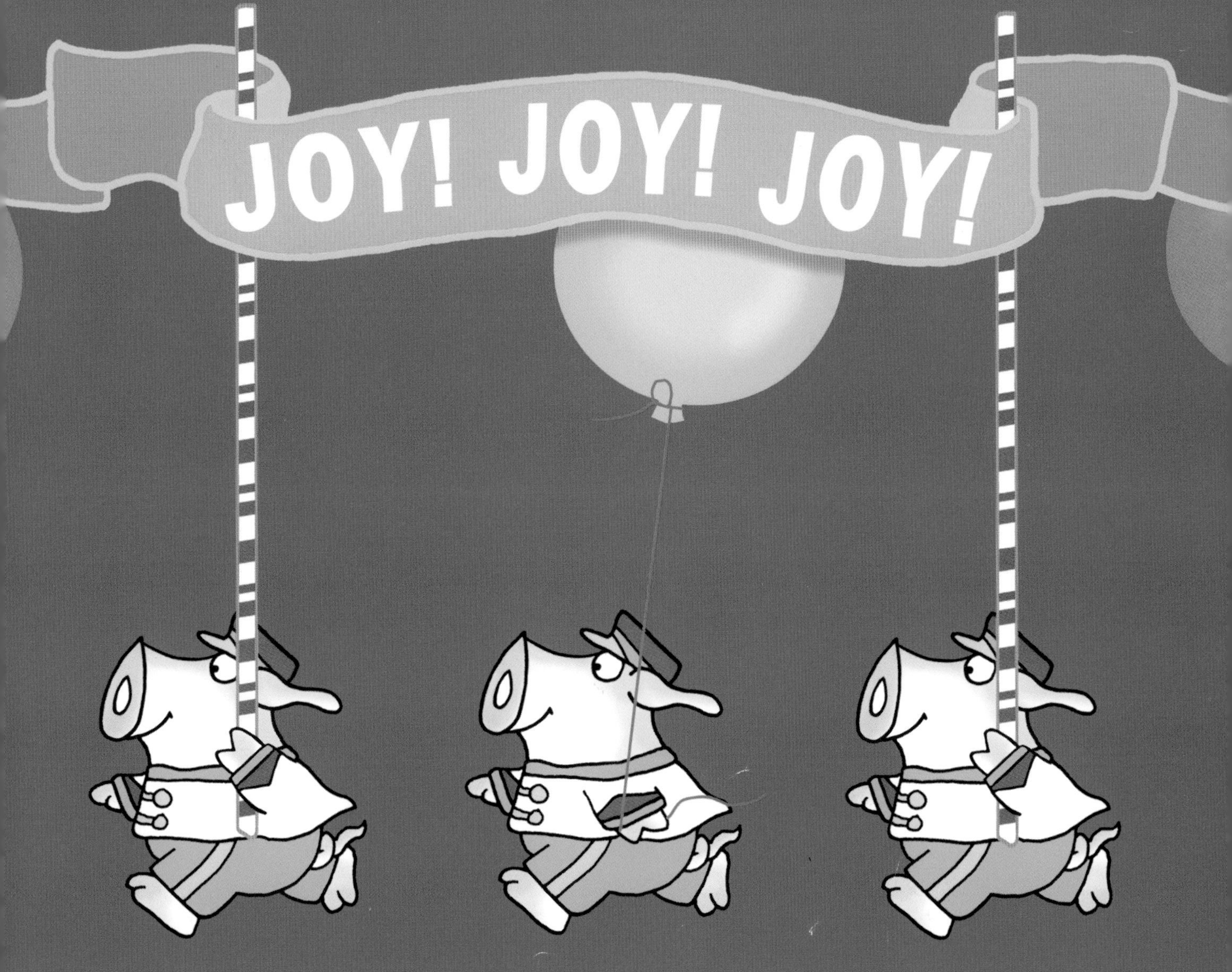
JOY! JOY! JOY!

Oh look! Drumming hippos,

14

with a **RAT-A-TAT-TAT.**

And even MORE hippos.

And one
drummer cat.

THE CHRISTMAS PARADE!

With holly confetti!
The Christmas Parade!
Here comes more!

Are you ready?

One
Santa
Claus
rhino!

Two cow saxophones!

Three piccolo mice!

And four ducks with trombones!

And then, last of all,
comes the TINIEST BIRD
with the

LOUDEST

tuba
you ever
have heard.

The parade is now over.
It's starting to snow.

And then...

DING DONG!

KNOCK KNOCK.

Is it someone
we know?

Go to the door.

Open it wide.

Look who it is
standing outside!

LETTERS

We thank you for watch-ing. Our time here is through.

MERRY CHRISTMAS

The End

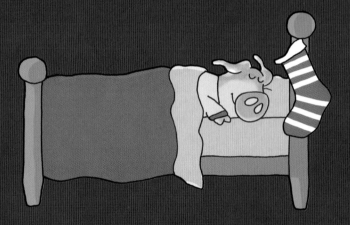